The Kingdom of Wrenly

8

The Secret World of Mermaids

By Jordan Quinn

Illustrated by Robert McPhillips

LITTLE SIMON

New York   London   Toronto   Sydney   New Delhi

LITTLE SIMON

An imprint of Simon & Schuster Children's Publishing Division
1230 Avenue of the Americas, New York, New York 10020
First Little Simon paperback edition May 2015
Copyright © 2015 by Simon & Schuster, Inc.
Also available in a Little Simon hardcover edition.
All rights reserved, including the right of reproduction in whole or in part in any form.
LITTLE SIMON is a registered trademark of Simon & Schuster, Inc., and associated colophon is a trademark of Simon & Schuster, Inc.
For information about special discounts for bulk purchases, please contact Simon & Schuster Special Sales at 1-866-506-1949 or business@simonandschuster.com.
The Simon & Schuster Speakers Bureau can bring authors to your live event. For more information or to book an event contact the Simon & Schuster Speakers Bureau at 1-866-248-3049 or visit our website at www.simonspeakers.com.
Manufactured in the United States of America 0415 FFG
2 4 6 8 10 9 7 5 3 1
Library of Congress Cataloging-in-Publication Data
Quinn, Jordan.
The secret world of mermaids / by Jordan Quinn ; illustrated by Robert McPhillips. — First Little Simon edition.
pages cm. — (The kingdom of Wrenly ; 8)
Summary: Lucas and Clara are floating on a raft when a wave casts them into the sea, where Lucas catches a glimpse of a coral kindom and a dark-haired mermaid helps him, but when his father, King Caleb, hears of this, he scolds Lucas and tells him he has broken an age-old pact.
ISBN 978-1-4814-3122-4 (pbk : alk. paper) — ISBN 978-1-4814-3123-1 (hc : alk. paper) — ISBN 978-1-4814-3124-8 (ebook) [1. Mermaids—Fiction. 2. Friendship—Fiction. 3. Princes—Fiction. 4. Kings, queens, rulers, etc.—Fiction.] I. McPhillips, Robert, illustrator. II. Title.
PZ7.Q31945Sf 2015
[Fic]—dc23
2014036040

CONTENTS

CHAPTER 1

My Turn

Swish! Swish! Swish! Prince Lucas and his best friend, Clara, swept dirt, leaves, and bits of straw into a corner of Ruskin's lair. They wanted the cave to be clean and perfect when Ruskin returned. Ruskin was on the island of Crestwood for the week. He was perfecting his fire-breathing skills, and Grom, the wizard overseeing Ruskin's training,

had told Lucas that being around
other dragons every once in a while
was good for him.

"Look at all the cobwebs!" cried
Clara, pointing to shadowy corners
of the lair.

"This place looks more like a

home for spiders than for a dragon,"
said Lucas.

They turned their brooms upside
down and began to brush the webs
from the corners of the lair. Spiders
scurried into the cracks between the
stones.

"I can't wait until Ruskin can go on more adventures with us," Lucas said.

"Me too," agreed Clara. "I wonder what land we'll discover next."

"Well, wherever it is," answered Lucas, "*I'm* going to be the one to discover it!"

Clara stopped sweeping the walls for a moment. "Why do you say it like *that*?" she asked.

Lucas shrugged. "I don't know. I guess it's because you always discover everything first," he said.

"I'm not trying to," responded Clara. "It's just because I know my way around the kingdom from all the bread deliveries I've done with my father."

"I know," said Lucas, "but I wish I could discover something before you just once."

Clara pulled a cobweb from her sleeve. "You're being silly," she said. "Besides, we've discovered lots of things *together.*"

"Like what?" questioned Lucas.

Clara thought for a moment. "How about the time we found the Breach in the Starless Forest—

remember?" she said. "We collected the healing vixberries for Ruskin!"

Lucas shook his head. "But don't forget it was *your* friend who showed us the Breach," he protested. "I would never have discovered it if it weren't for you!"

"Why does that matter?" asked Clara.

"Because we never would have found the Breach and saved Ruskin's life if you hadn't been friends with Bren."

Clara rested her broom against the wall. She didn't want her best friend to be upset with her, even if it was for a silly reason.

"Well, don't worry," she said,

pulling off a cobweb. "I know you'll uncover many mysteries before me. Just keep your eyes open."

Lucas nodded. "You bet I will," he said.

CHAPTER 2

The Raft

"What do you want to do today?" asked Clara as the two friends met on the palace steps.

"Discover a new land," said Lucas.

Clara rolled her eyes.

"Besides that," she said.

Lucas looked toward the water. "Want to build a sand castle?" he suggested.

Clara smiled. "Now, that's more

like it!" she said.

Lucas and Clara walked to Mermaid's Cove and worked on a sand castle all morning.

The tide had nearly reached the castle. Lucas dug a path from the moat to the edge of the water.

Seawater quickly began to fill the moat. Lucas plopped two hermit crabs onto the drawbridge.

"The hermit crabs will protect the sand castle from enemies," said Lucas.

"Good idea," said Clara as she stuck a sand dollar above the castle entrance. "What shall we call our castle?" she asked.

Lucas looked at their creation. The sand sparkled in the sun. The hermit crabs scuttled toward the moat. Small pieces of coral stood around the castle like leafless trees.

"How about Coral Castle?" he suggested.

Clara smiled and brushed loose strands of hair from her face with the back of her hand. "That's perfect," she said. She began to roll up

her pants. "Now let's go cool off."

"Right behind you!" said Lucas.

The waves rolled over their feet as they walked along the water. Then Lucas noticed something sticking out of some seaweed farther down the shore.

"What's that?" he said, pointing
at the tangled green mess.

The children ran down the beach
to see what the sea had washed up.

"It's a raft!" exclaimed Lucas.

They freed the raft from the seaweed. It was made from several rows
of narrow logs tied together with
ropes.

"It looks pretty strong," said Lucas.
"Let's take it out!"

Clara looked at the water. "We'd
better not," she said. "The waves look
kind of big."

"We can handle it," said Lucas. "Besides, it'll be so much fun!"

"What will we use for paddles?" asked Clara.

"I'll find some!" Lucas said.

Then he raced to another pile of seaweed and poked around. He quickly came back with two long pieces of driftwood and laid them on top of the raft.

"Ready to cast off!" he cried, dragging the

raft into the shallow water.

The raft bobbed up and down in the waves. Clara picked up one of the pieces of driftwood and carefully climbed on board.

"I'm not sure about this," she mumbled.

CHAPTER 3

Man Overboard

Lucas and Clara sat on the raft and paddled away from Mermaid's Cove. They passed a line of pelicans fishing in the water. Playful waves splashed against the sides of the raft. Lucas yanked a clump of seaweed from between the logs and tossed it into the water. Then he continued paddling.

This raft sure feels nice and sturdy,

he thought. *And these driftwood paddles are perfect too.* He looked out to sea and smiled proudly. He hadn't discovered a new land or anything, but at least he and his best friend were out having a fun adventure anyway.

They paddled over a coral
reef. Schools of colorful fish
swam beneath them. A seal
playfully poked his head above
the water and quickly disappeared
back under. Lucas and Clara
giggled.

Beyond the reef, the waves began to get bigger. Seawater sloshed over the sides of the raft and soaked their clothes. The farther out they went, the bigger the waves got. The little raft bobbed up and down. The salt water splashed their faces.

"I think we should turn around!" Clara shouted over the wind and waves.

But Lucas didn't hear his friend's cry. Something else had caught his attention.

"Look up ahead!" he shouted, pointing with his paddle. "A pod of dolphins!"

Clara stopped paddling, and together, they watched the dolphins leap high into the air and dive back into the water. *Splish! Splash!* The

dolphin show lasted several min-
utes. Neither of the children noticed
as the wind blew the raft farther out
to sea.

Clara looked back at the beach.
It had gotten very far away.

"Lucas, we need to turn back

NOW!" Clara cried. "We've gone too far out, and the waves are getting rough."

This time Lucas paid attention to his friend.

"You're right!" he called back. "If

we paddle on the same side, we'll be able to turn around."

Lucas and Clara paddled as hard as they could, but the raft barely turned at all.

"It's not working!" cried Clara.

"Keep paddling!" Lucas shouted.

They got up on their knees so they could paddle harder. The waves pushed against the raft. It rocked this way and that. Then a very large wave made the children lose their balance. They tumbled into the water. Clara quickly grabbed the side of the raft with both hands and climbed back on. Then she looked for her friend, but she didn't see him.

"Lucas?" she called. "Lucas!"

She watched the paddles drift

away on the waves. "LUCAS!" she
yelled. "WHERE ARE YOU?"

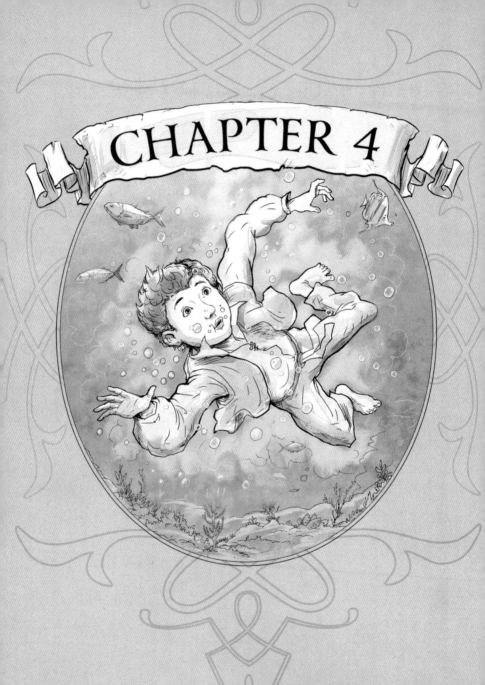

CHAPTER 4

Under the Sea

Lucas plunged deep into the sea. The water bubbled past him as he sank below the surface. Down and down he went. He opened his eyes as he fell, and what he saw was enchanting. There, on the ocean floor, stood a magical kingdom made of shimmering coral.

I must be dreaming, he thought.

He stared at the glittering towers,

arches, and bridges beneath him. He noticed a young mermaid with long, flowing black hair peeking out from behind one of the windows.

His mouth dropped open. *This must be the kingdom of the mermaids!* he exclaimed to himself. The mermaid girl smiled at him. Lucas tried to smile back, but he needed to get to the surface—and fast. He was running out of air!

He spied the bottom of the raft and began to swim toward it. It suddenly looked very far

away. Then he felt something grab
his arm. And there, next to him, was
the mermaid girl from the window.
She flicked her tail and swam Lucas
back to the world above. As soon as
his head broke the surface, he heard
Clara's cries.

"Lucas!" shouted Clara when she saw her friend.

Lucas grabbed hold of the raft. His clothes felt heavy as he pulled himself on board.

"Oh, thank goodness!" she cried. "Are you okay?"

"I think so," Lucas said, gasping for breath.

Then he looked toward the shore. Mermaid's Cove was almost completely out of sight.

"We need to get back before we lose sight of the mainland," he said. "Let's lie down on our stomachs and paddle with our hands."

They both lay down and paddled
like sea turtles. The little raft began
to move forward. Then it began to
pick up speed.

"We're moving faster than we're
paddling!" shouted Clara.

"Something must be pushing us!"
Lucas shouted back.

"Maybe it's a dolphin!" Clara said.

"Maybe," said Lucas. *Or a mermaid,* he thought.

The raft slowed down as they approached the beach. Lucas looked over his shoulder. He thought he saw a mermaid tail flash in the sun and then disappear underwater.

The children jumped off the raft and walked the rest of the way to shore. Then they plopped down onto the wet sand to catch their breath.

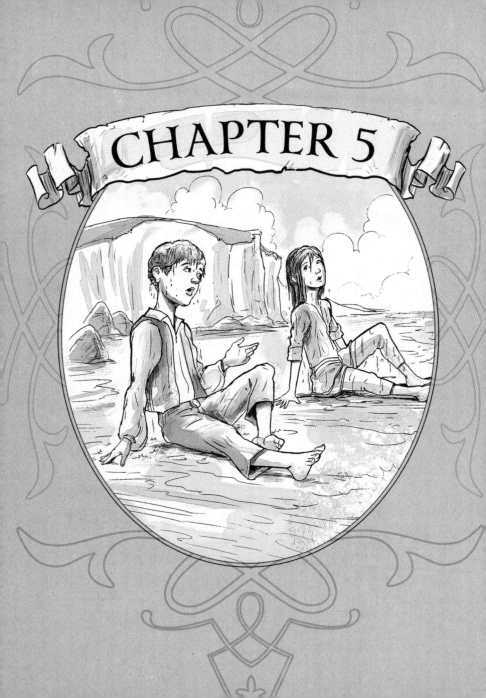

CHAPTER 5

A Fishy Tale

"Are you okay?" Clara asked again as she propped herself up.

Lucas nodded. "I'm sorry, Clara," he said. "I should have listened to you."

"That's okay," said his friend, squinting at the sun. "But you had me terrified!" she went on. "It felt like you were underwater forever."

Lucas wrung some seawater

from his wet shirt. "Really? I wish I could have stayed longer." He sighed. "You're never going to believe what I saw down there," he said.

Clara's eyes grew wide. "What do you mean?" she asked. She leaned over excitedly.

"I saw something amazing and magical," he said. "I saw the Mermaid Kingdom!"

Clara's jaw dropped. "But that's

impossible!" she declared. "Everyone says that the Mermaid Kingdom is hidden from human sight."

"I know!" agreed Lucas. "But I'm telling you, I *saw* it! And it was the most incredible thing I've ever seen."

Then he tried to describe the sparkling coral kingdom and the mermaid girl who had rescued him.

"I think she helped us

get back to shore too," Lucas added.

Clara shook her head in disbelief. "But I sit here in Mermaid's Cove more than anyone else and *I've* never even seen a mermaid. Not even the tip of a tail!" she said. "Are you sure you're not making this up?"

"Why would I do that?" asked Lucas.

"Well, I don't know," Clara went on. "Maybe because you wanted so badly to discover something first. It's just hard to believe that you happened to find an *entire kingdom* the very next day. . . ."

"I see your point," said Lucas, "but I promise I'm *not* making this up."

Clara watched the waves crash and foam on the shore.

"Well, all I can say is that I'm really glad you're safe," she said.

Lucas smiled at his friend and

sighed. He was too tired to try to convince her anymore today.

"I'm really glad we're *both* safe," he said.

And he left it at that.

CHAPTER 6

An Ancient Pact

Lucas walked Clara home and then headed for the palace. He snuck in through the kitchen only to find his father, King Caleb, grabbing an apple from the fruit bowl.

The king glanced over at his son. Lucas's clothes were still dripping wet, and there were bits of sand on his face.

"Good heavens, boy! What have

you been up to now?" cried the king.

Lucas shrugged as if it were no big deal. "Clara and I went swimming at Mermaid's Cove," he answered.

"With all your clothes on?" questioned his father.

Lucas wondered if he should tell the king what had happened. He didn't want to get in trouble, but he also wanted to ask his father about the

Mermaid Kingdom. He decided to tell the truth.

"Actually, we found a raft washed up on the beach," Lucas began. "And we paddled out into the cove."

The king raised an eyebrow.

"It was really fun," Lucas went on, "until the waves got too big . . .

and we kind of fell overboard."

"Kind of?" the king asked. "How do you *kind of* fall overboard?"

The prince shrugged. The king's

frown deepened.
Lucas knew what
was coming next.

"Lucas!" his
father bellowed.
"You are the heir
to the throne!
How could you
be so careless with
your safety?"

Lucas looked down
at his feet. "I'm very
sorry," he mumbled.

The king pointed out the window toward the distant water. "The

current is powerful," he went on. "You could have been swept out to sea!"

"I *promise* I'll be more careful from now on," Lucas said. Then he paused for a moment while his father calmed down. "But there's a little bit more. . . ."

The king's eyebrows rose and his brow wrinkled.

"Something strange happened when I was underwater."

"Go on," said the king.

So, Lucas told his father about how he had seen the kingdom of the

mermaids and how the mermaid girl had helped him.

The king shook his head in disbelief. "Lucas, do you realize that the mermaid broke an ancient pact to help you?" he asked.

Lucas shook his head. He had no idea what his father was talking about.

"Long ago the mermaids made a

pact with the kingdom of Wrenly to keep out of sight of humans," said the king. "And in return we give them their privacy."

Lucas knew the mermaids never showed themselves, but he didn't know it was because of an ancient agreement with Wrenly. Either way, it didn't stop him from wanting to

find out more about the mermaids.

"Well, now that I've *seen* a mermaid," said Lucas, "may I go back and explore their kingdom?"

"Did you not hear what I just said?" questioned his father. "Our

promise is to honor the mermaids'
privacy. And the answer to your
question is *no*."

Lucas kicked the stone floor with
his wet boot.

CHAPTER 7

Dreamweaver

Lucas blew out the candle on his nightstand and snuggled under his feather bed cover. The moonlight twinkled on the water outside his window. He couldn't stop thinking about the mermaids.

Soon he began to dream he was in the kingdom beneath the sea. He swam toward the coral castle. *Wow,* he thought. *I can breathe normally underwater.* He could see and hear, too. He glided to the castle door. Then he lifted the brass dolphin door knocker.

Boom! Boom! Boom! The sound echoed through the water.

Soon the door opened and the same mermaid with the long, flowing black hair answered the door. This time she wore her dark hair in a thick braid. A circlet of sea flowers crowned her head. She looked about the same age as Lucas.

"Hello, Prince Lucas," she said, shutting the door behind her and

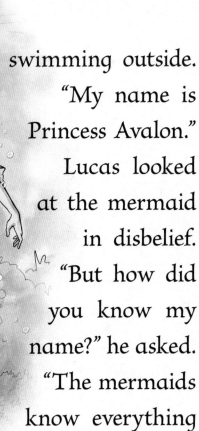

swimming outside. "My name is Princess Avalon." Lucas looked at the mermaid in disbelief. "But how did you know my name?" he asked. "The mermaids know everything about Wrenly," said the girl. "We may be hidden, but we like to watch and listen."

Lucas had so many questions, but

first he thanked
Avalon for
rescuing him.

Avalon bit
her lip shyly. "I
broke a pretty
big rule to save
you," she said.
"But how could I
not help the prince
of Wrenly?"

Lucas smiled. "Well, if it makes
you feel any better, I got in *big* trouble
when I got home," he added.

Avalon laughed. "Well, if we're

already both in trouble, then we might as well have fun!" she declared. "Would you like to take a look around and explore with me?"

The prince's face lit up.

The mermaid princess showed him around the castle and the royal gardens. They played hide-and-seek in a forest of seaweed. It was so tall

and thick that it felt like a maze.
Then they rested in a gazebo.

"Do you have any friends?" Lucas
asked.

"Of course I do!" said Avalon. "But they're all hiding."

"From what?" Lucas questioned.

"From *you*," she answered.

Lucas wanted to know why, but someone started calling his name.

"Lu-u-u-cas!" the voice called. "Lucas, WAKE UP!"

A bright light suddenly blinded him. Lucas squinted and blinked his eyes open. His mother pulled back another long curtain, and bright sunlight filled his bedroom.

"Time to get up," she said. "Clara's here."

Clara's mother, Anna Gills, was the royal seamstress. Clara often came to the castle with her mother—that's how she and Lucas had first met.

Lucas rubbed his eyes and stretched.

"I'll be down in a minute," he groaned.

He watched his mother leave the room. Then he frowned and rested his chin in his hand, thinking. *Darn!* he said to himself. *It was only a dream.*

CHAPTER 8

Breakfast in the Branches

"Have you eaten?" asked Lucas.

"Not yet," Clara said.

"Good," said the prince. "Let's have breakfast in the new royal tree fort."

Clara nodded excitedly.

The two friends loved to spend time in the royal tree fort. They played games there and had secret conversations. They called it the *new*

royal tree fort because Ruskin had
burned down the first one. Now,
after much training, Ruskin had better control over his fire breathing—
and Lucas had a new tree fort.

The children went down into
the kitchen and asked Cook to help
them with their picnic. They packed

blueberry muffins, butter, peaches, and two small glass containers of milk in a basket. He added cloth napkins and a butter knife. Then the children walked the well-worn path to the tree house. At the bottom of the tree, Lucas tied the basket to a pulley. He used the pulley to

hoist things up and down from the tree house. Clara yanked the rope, and up went the basket. Then Lucas climbed the wooden ladder nailed to the side of the trunk.

Clara followed behind. As soon as she got to the top, she poured herself a glass of milk and hopped up on the table. The cook had prepared them a proper morning feast.

"I had the craziest dream last night," Lucas said as he buttered a muffin.

Clara placed a napkin in her lap. "What was it about?" she asked.

"It was about the Mermaid Kingdom," he said. "And it seemed *so* real."

"Just like when you fell over-board?" asked Clara with a slight smirk on her face.

"Yes!" Lucas exclaimed. "Only this time I could breathe underwater! And I could see! And hear, too!"

Clara sipped her milk and set it down on the table. "That's pretty amazing," she said without much excitement. "So what happened?"

"I met the mermaid princess who rescued me after I fell off the raft," Lucas said. "She called herself Avalon."

Clara raised her eyebrows. "Avalon, huh? Well, that's a very nice name," she said. Then she took a bite of her muffin.

Lucas could tell Clara still didn't believe that he'd seen a mermaid, let alone been rescued by one.

But he went on with his story anyway.

"She showed me the royal gardens, and we played hide-and-seek in a seaweed maze."

"Wow, Lucas, you sure have a great imagination," Clara said.

Lucas smiled. "I do," he said with pride. "I bet I have the best imagination in all of Wrenly!" Then he frowned. "But I'm not making up what happened yesterday!"

Clara gave a shrug and smiled. "Well, who knows," she said. "Maybe your 'new friend,' Avalon, will be able to help you prove it."

Lucas's face brightened a little. "That's a good idea!"

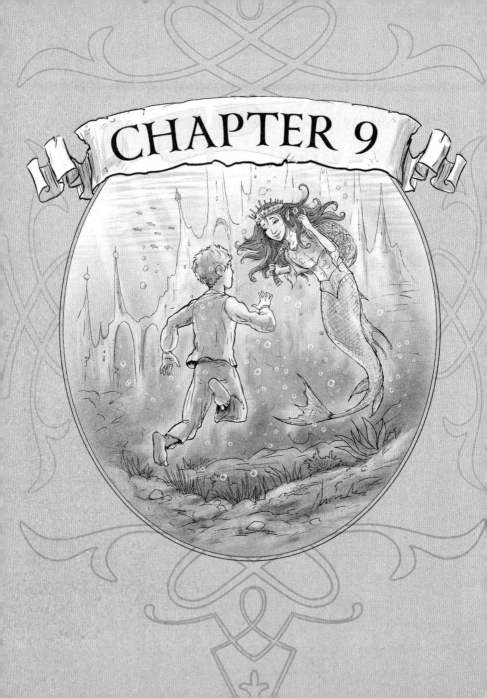

CHAPTER 9

Shell Collectors

That night Lucas dreamed about the underwater kingdom again.

"Follow me!" beckoned Avalon.

She waited for Lucas to catch up to her. This time her long, dark hair floated freely in the water. She held a sack over her shoulder.

Lucas swam toward Avalon in his bedclothes and bare feet. A school of fish parted to make way for him.

Then the two friends swam side by side. They passed a graceful manta ray and an old sea turtle. They glided under the bottom of a great ship. They dove closer to the ocean floor. Lucas could see ripples on the sand below. He noticed a coral reef up ahead.

"Help me collect shells!" Avalon said. She reached into her bag and handed him a net made of woven seaweed. "Sometimes the waves push shells into the reef. You'll find them in the nooks and crannies."

"It's like a treasure hunt!" exclaimed Lucas.

Avalon nodded. Lucas swam to the reef and began to search for shells. He found a calico scallop, a lion's paw, and a striped moon shell.

Inside the mouth of a small cave, he uncovered a lightning whelk and something else very rare.

"Look!" Lucas cried. "I found a morning glory of the sea!"

Avalon swam over.

"It's beautiful!" she exclaimed.

"My friend Clara has always

wanted to find one of these."

"Why don't we leave it for her at Mermaid's Cove?" Avalon suggested. "I'll show you where when we're done."

Lucas nodded. Maybe this would be the perfect way to prove to Clara that this was all real. "Avalon, you're a genius!"

When their seaweed nets were full, Lucas followed Avalon to Mermaid's Cove. They hid the shells on the beach behind Turtle Rock.

"Where are we going next, Avalon?" asked Lucas.

But Avalon didn't answer. Lucas turned around. He looked in every direction, but the mermaid princess was gone.

"Avalon?" he called. "AVALON!"

The sound of his own voice woke him up. He looked out the window at the ocean.

"Darn!" Lucas said out loud. "It was just another dream!"

This time he halfheartedly tossed his pillow against the wall.

CHAPTER 10

A Lesson in Friendship

"Father, I keep having these dreams that seem so real," Lucas began as he sat down to breakfast. His mother had left early for Primlox, the island of the fairies, so he and his father were alone at the table.

"About what?" asked his father.

"The Mermaid Kingdom," he said. "I met a mermaid princess named Avalon, and we became friends."

The king raised an eyebrow.

Lucas helped himself to a sweet roll from a platter on the table.

"I dreamed about her again last night," he went on. "And then *poof!* I woke up and she was gone. It really stinks!"

His father pierced a sausage with his fork and looked over at the frustrated prince.

"Well, now you know why we have a pact with the mermaids," said his father.

"What do you mean by that?" Lucas questioned.

"You see, whenever a human and a mermaid become friends, it always ends in disappointment," his father said. "Being friends with a

mermaid is always too hard."

Lucas dropped his sweet roll.

"But that's the silliest reason for a pact I've ever heard!" he said in disbelief.

His father looked at him in surprise.

"All my friendships have been hard at first," Lucas went on, "but they were all worth fighting for."

"Go on," urged his father, wiping his mouth with his napkin. He leaned back in his chair.

"Look at my friendship with

Clara," said Lucas. "At first you said we couldn't be friends, but I got you to change your mind, and now she's like a member of our family."

"True," said the king thoughtfully.

"And then there's Ruskin," Lucas went on. "He burned everything up

and made a mess of the castle."

His father nodded and frowned at the memories.

"But now that Ruskin's gotten some training, he's becoming the pride of the kingdom—not to mention my closest friend."

The king sighed and stroked his red beard.

"You've become very wise, Lucas," said his father. "A good friendship *is* worth fighting for, and guarding against disappointment does seem a silly reason to have a pact." His father leaned over and whispered, "To tell you the truth, I'm not even certain who made the pact in the first place. Perhaps I'll take up this matter with Avalon's father, King Zane."

Lucas's eyes grew wide.

"You know Avalon?" he asked. "Are you saying my dreams might be *real*?"

"I've never met Avalon," said the

king, "but I know King Zane has a daughter. As for your dreams, they may have been the princess's way of showing you her kingdom without further breaking the pact. After all, the mermaids do have some magic."

Lucas suddenly jumped up from the table.

"Father, may I please be excused?" he asked. "I have to go to Clara's."

"What's the big hurry?" asked his father.

"I'll tell you later!" said Lucas as he ran from the dining room.

CHAPTER 11

A Gift from the Sea

Lucas ran all the way to the bakery and got Clara. She had just finished bagging fresh bread with her father.

"Come on!" he cried. "I have to show you something at the cove!"

On the way Lucas told Clara about the dream he'd had the night before, and how he'd left a morning glory of the sea shell for Clara behind Turtle Rock.

"Will you believe me if we find a shell there?" asked Lucas.

Clara didn't have to think twice about her answer. "Definitely!" she said.

Clara knew how rare it was to find a morning glory of the sea shell. They were cone-shaped with a bottom that delicately fanned out like the petals of a morning glory flower. Although the outside was a plain cream color,

the inside edges were a bright royal blue that faded to a golden yellow. Lucas's parents kept the only one that had ever been found in a glass case in the library.

They stopped in front of Turtle Rock.

"Go ahead," said Lucas, crossing his fingers. He really hoped that the shell would be there. "Take a look."

Clara peeked behind the rock. Then she squealed with delight. "There *is* a morning glory of the sea shell!" she exclaimed.

She picked up the delicate cream

shell from the sand and looked at it
in wonder.

"I'm sorry I ever doubted you,"
she said. "Will you please forgive me
and tell me the whole story of the
mermaid princess again?"

"I'd love to!" said Lucas.

And that's just what he did.

As he was telling his story Lucas realized that the best part wasn't that he had discovered a new land before Clara—it was that he had discovered a new friend.

Hear ye! Hear ye!
Presenting the next book from
The Kingdom of Wrenly!
Here's a sneak peek!

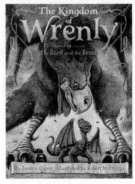

"Sir Archie won!" shouted Prince Lucas.

"No, Sir Fred won!" cried Clara.

"Squawk!" crowed Ruskin, Lucas's pet dragon. He was definitely on the prince's side.

"Okay, let's call it a *tie!*" Lucas said.

"No way!" argued Clara. "Sir Fred won fair and square!"

Excerpt from *The Bard and the Beast*

Prince Lucas and his best friend, Clara, had just had a toad race. They argued and laughed as they ran down the castle halls.

Then, all at once, Lucas's muddy leather boots skidded to a stop. Clara didn't see in time and bumped into Lucas. Ruskin smacked into the back of Clara's knees. Queen Tasha blocked the hallway. She tapped her black velvet shoe on the stone floor and stared disapprovingly at the mud-covered children.

"Where on earth have you been, Lucas?" she said sternly. "You're late for your first music lesson!"

Clara peeked out from behind Lucas. "Um, I'd better be going," she said uncomfortably. Then she turned and hurried toward the door.

The queen kept her eyes on her son. Lucas wiped some toad slime on his pants and sighed heavily.

"Come on, Mother," he complained. "You know I don't want to play a musical instrument!"

"It's not up for discussion," his mother said.

What had the prince gotten himself into this time?

Excerpt from *The Bard and the Beast*